Disney

MINNIE

Dr. Daisy, Pet Vet

Minnie Mouse rushed into Mickey Mouse's house bubbling with excitement.

"Isn't it wonderful, Mickey? Figaro is going to be a model for Pet Food Digest!"

"That's great Minnie," said Mickey. "How did he get the job?"

"It's a contest! I'm sending in photos! I just know Figaro will win!"

Mickey hoped Minnie was right, but he wasn't sure that Figaro was a model cat. He sure didn't listen to Mickey, or come when he was called.

"Is there a contest for dogs, too?" Mickey asked, "I know Pluto would be a great model!"

Mickey took some pictures of Pluto doing tricks.

"Oh boy!" said Mickey. "You and Figaro will be famous!"

Pluto and Figaro's photos looked great. Mickey and Minnie mailed them off, hoping for good news!

Two weeks went by, and Mickey had almost forgotten about the contest when he got a phone call from Pet Food Digest. Pluto and Figaro had both been chosen for a special pet photo shoot!

"Guess what, Minnie? Pet Food Digest is coming to take pictures of Figaro and Pluto tomorrow!"

The following morning, Pluto was up early waiting for the photographer. He was very excited about being in a photo shoot!

The photographer arrived with tons of equipment. Pluto couldn't wait to pose, but Figaro didn't like the fuss or the hot lights. He tried to lure Pluto away from the photographer with one of his favorite chew toys, but Pluto was annoyed.

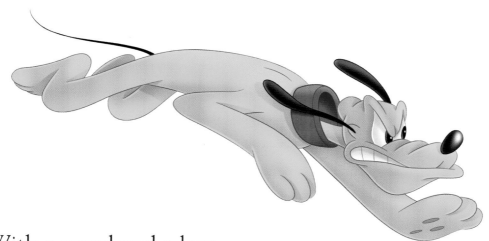

With a growl and a leap,
Pluto started chasing Figaro.

"Here, boy!" Mickey tried to get
Pluto's attention. "Be a good dog,
and I'll give you a nice bone!"

Pluto wasn't listening. He was too
busy trying to catch Figaro.

As Pluto and Figaro raced around the room, Pluto's tail knocked over the lights. Then Figaro leaped over the backdrop and it crashed to the floor! They faced off, hissing and growling, the photo shoot forgotten, as they fought for the chew toy.

Everyone was surprised, especially Figaro, when Pluto suddenly yelped.

"Pluto, are you okay?" cried Mickey.

"Figaro, did you scratch Pluto?" demanded Minnie.

Pluto held his nose and Figaro felt terrible! He hadn't meant to hurt Pluto.

"Well, we'd better get you to the vet," said Mickey. "Somebody should look at that scratch."

"How are we going to get an appointment on such short notice?" Mickey worried.

"Call Dr. Daisy. She takes care of all the animals for Pet Food Digest. I'm sure she'll be happy to see you right away!" said the photographer.

"Now Figaro," said Minnie, "apologize to Pluto! You know you are not allowed to scratch!"

Figaro was sorry. He hoped Dr. Daisy would make Pluto feel better.

Mickey phoned Dr. Daisy, and she said they could come right away. Pluto was excited. He liked to visit new people and places. His nose felt better just thinking about meeting Dr. Daisy!

Dr. Daisy cleaned the scratch on Pluto's nose and put some cream on it.

"There you go, Pluto!" she said, "Good as new! Now, just for my records, when was Pluto's last checkup?"

"Gosh…" said Mickey.

"Golly…" said Minnie.

"That long?" said Dr. Daisy. "Well, we'd better do one now!"

"But what about our photo shoot?" asked the photographer. "Why don't you take pictures while I do the checkup? A real visit to the vet would make a great article for Pet Food Digest!"

"Great idea!" the photographer said. He took pictures of Pluto getting weighed.

He took pictures of Pluto having his ears checked.

He took pictures as Dr. Daisy examined Pluto's teeth.

Then it was time for a shot. Pluto was scared.
"Poor Pluto!" said Mickey.

Mickey had a great idea. He gave Pluto a bone. Pluto was so happy he didn't even notice Dr. Daisy giving him the shot.

"See Pluto? That wasn't so bad!"

Minnie and Figaro came back to Dr. Daisy's a few weeks later.

"Isn't this a great article!" said Minnie, as she leafed through the new issue of Pet Food Digest. "I never knew how important it is to give your pets regular checkups!"

Figaro wasn't really looking forward to seeing Dr. Daisy, but he was determined to be on his best behavior.

Dr. Daisy said that Figaro was a very healthy cat. Figaro decided he was also a cat who was never going to touch Pluto's chew toys again!